Margaret Hillert's

Tom
Thumb

A Beginning-to-Read Book

Illustrated by Yu–Mei Han
retold story of Tom Thumb

NORWOOD HOUSE PRESS

DEAR CAREGIVER,

The books in this Beginning-to-Read collection may look somewhat familiar in that the original versions could have been a part of your own early reading experiences. These carefully written texts feature common sight words to provide your child multiple exposures to the words appearing most frequently in written text. These new versions have been updated and the engaging illustrations are highly appealing to a contemporary audience of young readers.

Begin by reading the story to your child, followed by letting him or her read familiar words and soon your child will be able to read the story independently. At each step of the way, be sure to praise your reader's efforts to build his or her confidence as an independent reader. Discuss the pictures and encourage your child to make connections between the story and his or her own life. At the end of the story, you will find reading activities and a word list that will help your child practice and strengthen beginning reading skills. These activities, along with the comprehension questions are aligned to current standards, so reading efforts at home will directly support the instructional goals in the classroom.

Above all, the most important part of the reading experience is to have fun and enjoy it!

Shannon Cannon

Shannon Cannon,
Literacy Consultant

Norwood House Press • www.norwoodhousepress.com
Beginning-to-Read™ is a registered trademark of Norwood House Press.
Illustration and cover design copyright ©2017 by Norwood House Press. All Rights Reserved.

Authorized adapted reprint from the U.S. English language edition, entitled Tom Thumb by Margaret Hillert. Copyright © 2017 Pearson Education, Inc. or its affiliates. Reprinted with permission. All rights reserved. Pearson and Tom Thumb are trademarks, in the US and/or other countries, of Pearson Education, Inc. or its affiliates. This publication is protected by copyright, and prior permission to re-use in any way in any format is required by both Norwood House Press and Pearson Education. This book is authorized in the United States for use in schools and public libraries.

Designer: Lindaanne Donohoe
Editorial Production: Lisa Walsh

LIBRARY OF CONGRESS CATALOGING-IN-PUBLICATION DATA
Names: Hillert, Margaret, author. I Han, Yu-Mei, illustrator.
Title: Tom Thumb / by Margaret Hillert ; illustrated by Yu-Mei Han.
Description: Chicago, IL : Norwood House Press, 2016. I Series: A Beginning-to-read book I Summary: "An easy format retelling of the classic fairy tale,Tom Thumb and the tiny boy's big adventures. Original edition revised with new illustrations. Includes reading activities and a word list"-- Provided by publisher.
Identifiers: LCCN 2015047814 (print) I LCCN 2016009562 (ebook) I ISBN 9781603579315 (ebook) I ISBN 9781599537900 (library edition : alk. paper) I ISBN 9781603579315 (eBook)
Subjects: I CYAC: Fairy tales. I Size--Folklore. I Folklore--England.
Classification: LCC PZ8.H5425 To 2016 (print) I LCC PZ8.H5425 (ebook) I DDC 398.2 [E] --dc23
LC record available at https://lccn.loc.gov/2015047814

288N—072016
Manufactured in the United States of America in North Mankato, Minnesota.

We want a little boy.
Little boys are fun.
Where can we get
a little boy?

Oh, look here!
Look in here!
Here is a little boy.
A little, little boy.

Good, good.
This is what I want.
I like this little one.

Mother, Mother.
Look where I am.
Come and get me.
Help! Help!

Oh, my. Oh, my.
How did you get
in here?
Come out. Come out.

And get in here.
Now see what you have to do.

Come with me now.
We will go out here.
We will walk and walk.
Look here.
Here is something big.

Oh, oh.
Here I go.
In, in, in.
Help, Mother!
Help!

Here you are.
You are out now.
You are here with me.

I am not with you now.
I am up here.
Up, up, up.

Now here I go down.
Down, down, down.
What can I do?

Oh, help! Help!
Something wants
to eat me.
Here I go.

And here I am.
But what is this?
Where am I?

Oh, look. Look.
Here is a little, little boy.
I want this boy.

Here is something
for you.
Sit down on it.
Sit here with me.
I like you.

And I like to ride.
It is fun to ride.
Here is something for you
to ride, too.

This is fun.
I like to do this.
I like to ride and ride.

But I want to go away
now.
I want to see my mother
and my father.

Here is something for you.
It is something good
to have.
Take it with you.

Oh, this is good.
But it is so big.
It makes me work.
Work, work, work.

Here I am, Mother and Father.
Look what I have.
It is for you.
It will help you.

Foundational Skills

In addition to reading the numerous high-frequency words in the text, this book also supports the development of foundational skills.

Phonological Awareness: The /th/ sound

Oral Blending: Say the beginning and ending sounds of the following words and ask your child to listen to the sounds and say the whole word:

/th/ + ink = think	/th/ + in = thin	/th/ + umb = thumb
/th/ + ing = thing	/th/ + imble = thimble	/th/ + ick = thick
/th/ + ank = thank	/th/ + ump = thump	/th/ + ird = third

Phonics: The letter Tt

1. Demonstrate how to form the letters **T** and **t** for your child.
2. Have your child practice writing **T** and **t** at least three times each.
3. Ask your child to point to the words in the book that start with the letter **t**.
4. Write down the following words and ask your child to circle the letter **t** in each word:

three	not	the	thumb	kitten	with
father	little	want	with	tap	sit
kite	top	Tom	two	take	this

Fluency: Choral Reading

1. Reread the story with your child at least two more times while your child tracks the print by running a finger under the words as they are read. Ask your child to read the words he or she knows with you.
2. Reread the story aloud together. Be careful to read at a rate that your child can keep up with.
3. Repeat choral reading and allow your child to be the lead reader and ask him or her to change from a whisper to a loud voice while you follow along and change your voice.

Language

The concepts, illustrations, and text help children develop language both explicitly and implicitly.

Vocabulary: Synonyms

1. Write the following words on separate pieces of paper:

   | little | miniature | tiny | wee | bitty | teeny |
   | huge | gigantic | large | enormous | colossal | immense |

2. Read each word to your child and ask your child to repeat it. Explain whether the word means big or small.

3. Fold a sheet of paper in half lengthwise. Draw a line down the middle of the paper. Write the words **small** and **big** at the top each column.

4. Mix the words up. Point to a word and ask your child to read it. Provide clues if your child needs them. Ask your child to place the word in the correct column under the synonym for the word.

Reading Literature and Informational Text

To support comprehension, ask your child the following questions. The answers either come directly from the text or require inferences and discussion.

Key Ideas and Detail

- Ask your child to retell the sequence of events in the story.
- How does Tom Thumb take a bath?

Craft and Structure

- Is this a book that tells a story or one that gives information? How do you know?
- Do you think Tom Thumb was scared of the giant?

Integration of Knowledge and Ideas

- What things would you like to do if you were as small as Tom Thumb?
- What kinds of animals can give rides to people?

Tom Thumb uses the 60 words listed below.

This list can be used to practice reading the words that appear in the text. You may wish to write the words on index cards and use them to help your child build automatic word recognition. Regular practice with these words will enhance your child's fluency in reading connected text.

a	eat	I	oh	up
am		in	on	
and	Father	is	one	walk
are	for	it	out	want(s)
away	fun			we
		like	ride	what
big	get	little		where
boy(s)	go	look	see	will
but	good		sit	with
		makes	so	work
can	have	me	something	
come	help	Mother		you
	here	my	take	
do	how		this	
did		not	to	
down		now	too	

ABOUT THE AUTHOR Margaret Hillert has helped millions of children all over the world learn to read independently. She was a first grade teacher for 34 years and during that time started writing books that her students could both gain confidence in reading and enjoy. She wrote well over 100 books for children just learning to read. As a child, she enjoyed writing poetry and continued her poetic writings as an adult for both children and adults.

Photograph by Glenna Washburn

ABOUT THE ILLUSTRATOR Yu–Mei Han wanted to be an artist ever since she was a young girl. After she earned a fine arts degree from a university in her native Taiwan, she moved to The United States and studied at The School of Visual Arts and The Art Students League in New York City. She currently lives in Queens, New York with her husband. www.yumeihan.com